INDIA

MAJOR WORLD NATIONS
INDIA

John C. Caldwell

CHELSEA HOUSE PUBLISHERS
Philadelphia

Chelsea House Publishers

Copyright © 1999 by Chelsea House Publishers,
a division of Main Line Book Co.
All rights reserved.
Printed in Hong Kong

First Printing.

1 3 5 7 9 8 6 4 2

Library of Congress Cataloging-in-Publication Data

Caldwell, John C.q(John Cope), 1913-
India / John C. Caldwell.
p. cm. — (Major world nations)
Includes index.
Summary: Examines the history, people, geography, economy,
climate and culture of India.
ISBN 0-7910-4988-4 (hc)
1. India—Juvenile literature. [1. India.] I. Title.
II. Series.
DS407.C34 1998
954—dc21   98-15265
CIP
AC

ACKNOWLEDGEMENTS

The Publishers thank the following for permission to reproduce the illustrations in this
book:
Douglas Dickins; The Government of India; I.C.A.; Monitor Press Features; Oxfam;
Torge; U.S.I.S.

CONTENTS

AFGHANISTAN

Khyber Pass

Peshawar

River

Lahore

Sutlej

PAKISTAN

Indus

Indus River

GREAT INDIAN DESERT

Jodhpur

Delhi

New Delhi

Agra

Jumna R.

Kanpur

Ahmedabad

VINDHYA MTS.

Narbada

R.

Nagpur

DECCAN

THE

KASHMIR
(IN DISPUTE)

Srinagar

H I M A L A Y A

N O R T H I N D I A N P L A I N

Ganges R.

Lucknow

Patna

Ganges R.

Ranchi

Jamshedpur

MOUNTAINS

MT. Everest

NEPAL

SIKKIM

BHUTAN

Brahmaputra R.

ASSAM

BANGLADESH

Dacca

Calcutta

CHINA

TIBET

MYANMAR

Mandalay

Irrawaddy River

Rangoon

Bombay
(Mumbai)

Godavari

River

Hyderabad

Kistna

R.

EASTERN GHATS

WESTERN GHATS

Bangalore

Madras

Calicut

TAMIL
LAND

Arabian Sea

Bay of
Bengal

Andaman
Islands

Nicobar
Islands

SUMATRA

SRI
LANKA

Colombo

Indian Ocean

MILES
0   200   400
0   300   600
KILOMETRES

30°

20°

10°

70°   80°   90°

Don Pitcher

FACTS AT A GLANCE

Land and People

Official Name India

Location Asia, surrounded by the Arabian Sea to the west, the Bay of Bengal to the east and the Himalayas to the north.

Area 1,269,214 square miles (3,287,263 square kilometers)

Climate Due to the vast area of the country, the climate differs from the north to the south. India has a three season year—hot, wet and cool.

Capital Delhi

Other Cities Mumbai (Bombay), Calcutta, Bangalore

Population 968 million

Population Density 792 persons per square mile (306 persons per square kilometer)

Major Rivers Indus, Ganges

Mountains Himalayas

Languages Eighteen languages are recognized, and they fall into two major groups: Indo-Aryan and Dravidian. There is no official language.

Religions	Hinduism, Buddhism, Islam, Sikhism, Jainism, Zoroastrianism, Christianity
Literacy Rate	54 percent
Average Life Expectancy	59 years for males, 60 years for females

Economy

Natural Resources	Coal, petroleum
Agricultural Products	Rice, wheat, coconuts, tea, coffee, spices
Industries	Textile, film, manufacturing
Major Imports	Oil, petroleum products, non-electrical machinery
Major Exports	Textiles, engineering goods, marine products, grains, computer software
Currency	Rupee

Government

Form of Government	Parliamentary (multiparty)
Government Bodies	Lower House (House of the People) and an Upper House (Council of States)
Formal Head of State	President
Head of Government	Prime Minister
Voting Rights	All Indians over the age of eighteen have the right to vote

HISTORY AT A GLANCE

2500 B.C. Harappa and Mohenjodaro, two of the world's first cities, are built by a civilization in the Indus Valley.

1500 B.C. The Aryans, or Indo-Europeans, invade India from the northwest.

1200 B.C. The *Vedas*, the earliest Hindu texts, are composed.

800-400 B.C. The *Upanishads*, Hindu religious texts, are composed.

500 B.C. Two new religions, Buddhism and Jainism, are founded.

326 B.C. Alexander the Great is forced to turn back before invading India.

321 B.C. The Maurya Empire is founded in northern India.

262 B.C. The Maurya Emperor Asoka converts to Buddhism and makes it the state religion.

232 B.C. Asoka dies and the Maurya Empire soon dissolves (184 B.C.).

320 A.D. After years of division the Gupta Empire unites

9

northern India. The Gupta period is one of great artistic and literary accomplishments.

350   The invasion of India by the Huns is repulsed, but weakens the Guptas, who are finally overthrown in 480.

850   The Chola Dynasty is founded, and over the next two centuries controls southern India, Ceylon, and parts of Malaya and Indonesia.

1207   Muslim invaders create the Sultanate of Delhi.

1398   Tartar invaders under Tamerlane defeat a large Muslim army and destroy Delhi.

1469   Birth of the Guru Nanak, who founds the Sikh religion.

1498   Portuguese navigator Vasco da Gama sails around Africa and reaches India's southwestern coast.

1510   The Portuguese capture Goa, a small but prosperous enclave they continue to occupy until 1961.

1526   Babar, claiming descent from both Tamerlane and Genghis Khan, overthrows the Sultan of Delhi and founds a new Muslim dynasty, the Mughals.

1556-1605   The reign of Akbar, the greatest of the Mughals.

1627-1658   The reign of Shah Jahan, the Mughal emperor whose extravagant building program includes the construction of the Taj Mahal.

1640   The British establish their first base in India, near Madras, which serves as the headquarters of the British East India Company.

1757	British and native forces under Robert Clive defeat a large army of Indian and French troops (June 23) at Plassey.
1800-1805	The British break the power of the Mahrattas, the major remaining Hindu dynasty.
1845-1849	In two wars (1845-1846, 1848-1849) the British defeat the Sikhs and establish control of northwestern India.
1857	In a revolt called the Indian Mutiny, native troops rebel against foreign rule (May 10), marking the beginning of the modern independence movement.
1858	After suppression of the Mutiny, Britain assumes direct rule of India and dissolves the East India Company.
1919	A movement of non-violent resistance to British rule begins. Troops under British command fire on demonstrators in Amritsar (April 13), killing 379 and wounding 1,208.
1920	Mohandas "Mahatma" Gandhi leads his first major non-violence campaign. This leads to his imprisonment by the British (1922-1924).
1930	Mahatma Gandhi leads a massive non-violent resistance to the British salt tax.
1947	British rule ends on August 14. Nehru becomes the first prime minister of independent India.
1948	Mahatma Gandhi is assassinated in New Delhi (January 30).
1961	Indian troops seize the Portuguese enclave of Goa, ending the last foreign presence in the

country.

1962 Border conflict with China over Himalayan frontier (October-November).

1965 War breaks out with West Pakistan over disputed Kashmir territory.

1966 Indira Gandhi, daughter of Jawaharlal Nehru, is elected prime minister.

1971 East Pakistan declares itself the independent nation of Bangladesh. India recognizes Bangladesh and clashes with Pakistan on its western border before a ceasefire goes into effect.

1975 Indira Gandhi declares a state of emergency and suspends some civil liberties. The resulting discontent causes her to be voted out in 1977.

1980 Indira Gandhi is re-elected, and embarks on a more radical program of social and economic reform.

1984 Indira Gandhi is assassinated by two of her Sikh bodyguards in retaliation for government attacks on Sikh separatists. She is succeeded by her son Rajiv.

1988 Rajiv Gandhi sends Indian troops to Sri Lanka (Ceylon) to intervene in a civil war between the Tamil and Sinhalese ethnic groups.

1989 While campaigning in a Tamil area of India, Rajiv Gandhi is assassinated. A long period of political instability follows.

1998 India detonates nuclear testing devices and increases tension with Pakistan.

1

Let's Visit India

People often think of India as a very strange country. The Indians, too, are thought to be "different" and to have peculiar customs which are difficult to understand. The sacred cow and the caste system, for example, are found only in India. But these differences are only a small part of the story. To know about India, we have to learn something of the living conditions of the Indian people and to try to understand their history and their hopes for the future. India is one of the oldest civilizations of the world. The forces which were active in her past are still there today and they have to be taken into account when we think of present-day India.

India is a huge and important country. The total population is in the region of 968,000,000. India has had great influence upon other countries in Asia. Indian culture and ideas have spread to every country in the East. It is interesting that Indian religions,

Hinduism and Buddhism, were taken to other nations without war or conquest; they moved abroad peacefully.

During recent years, India has become important for another reason. Since the end of the Second World War, the world has been divided. There were the communist nations, led by Russia(now known as the Commonwealth of Independent States), and there were the Western nations, led by the United States. Sometimes, as in Korea, the trouble between them has led to bitter fighting.

The United States and its allies believe that nations can remain free of communist control by joining together in military alliances. The government of India has refused to join either side and has become the leader of the neutralist nations. These are countries that believe it is possible to have the friendship of both Communist nations and Western nations. They are all in Asia and Africa, and have followed India's leadership.

Being a member of the British Commonwealth, India has close links with the United Kingdom and with the other Commonwealth nations. In spite of their different approach to world problems, they have maintained very friendly relations.

India is as interesting as it is important. It is a land of contrasts. Among its people are some of the richest men in the world, but millions are among the poorest, and more of them are always hungry than in any other country.

A large part of the population of India cannot read or write, but India has produced some of the world's greatest literature—

One of the many ancient temples in India.

and also the longest poem ever written, The *Mahabharata*. It has 700,000 words.

Millions of Indians live almost exactly as did their forefathers centuries ago. There are also big modern cities. India is a land of towering snow-capped mountains; it is also a land of jungles, deserts, and terrible heat. The wettest spot in the world is in India, and there are also areas that have almost no rainfall.

Another unusual fact about India, one which shows us that India has unusual problems to solve, is that there are eighteen major languages and over 1,600 different dialects. No one language is spoken by more than half the people. Major efforts have been made to adopt Hindi as the official language in India and to gradually phase out English.

Now let's learn more about India, its geography and climate, its people and their long history.

Carrying water from the village well.

2

The Land and the People

From the map on page 6, you will see that India is shaped like a triangle with the point, or apex, in the south. Or we can compare its shape to that of a big ice-cream cone. The broad top of the cone is cold and white with the snow of the world's highest mountains. These are the Himalayas. In these same mountains is the highest peak in the world, Mt. Everest, over 29,000 feet (8,848 meters) high, which lies outside India, on the boundary between Tibet and Nepal.

The mountains descend into jungle-covered hills, and the hills descend to the great North Indian Plain. This is the second of India's four main geographical regions. It extends from the Bay of Bengal in the east to the Arabian Sea in the west. This part of India is sometimes called Hindustan. It is the center of Indian culture and the part where most of the great cities are located. One language spoken here, Hindi, is one of the most important languages of India.

India's most important rivers flow through the North Indian Plain. They are the Ganges—with its main tributaries the Jumna and

17

The Himalayas, the world's highest mountains.

Gogra—and the Brahmaputra. From their sources in the Himalaya Mountains the Ganges and the Brahmaputra flow for great distances through India and then into Bangladesh, India's eastern neighbor.

The long Indus River is also very important to India but this river does not flow through India itself. It rises in the mountains of Tibet and then flows through the disputed territory of Kashmir into India's western neighbor, Pakistan. However, some of its tributaries are partly in India and India uses their water to irrigate much of the North Indian Plain.

The southern reaches of the North Indian Plain extend to the Vindhya Mountains. Southward again, another range slopes down to a great plateau—an area of land which is fairly flat, but well above sea-level. This plateau is called the Deccan. It stands at an average height of about 2,000 feet (610 meters) above the sea, and is the third of India's four main regions. To the east and the west, rugged

18

mountain ranges separate the Deccan from the sea. These are called *ghats*, meaning elevated places. The Western Ghats are in southwest India, between the Deccan and the Arabian Sea. The Eastern Ghats, not as rugged nor as high, lie between the Deccan and the Bay of Bengal.

Between the Ghats and the sea, there is the coastal plain of southern India, the fourth major geographical area. This flat area along the Arabian Sea and the Bay of Bengal broadens out in the south, to become what is sometimes called Tamil Land because the Indians who live there are called Tamils. The flat plains of Tamil Land extend to the very tip of the cone and continue to a point at Cape Comorin (Kanyakumari). To the south lies the big island of Sri Lanka, separated from India by seventy miles (over 112 kilometers) of island-dotted ocean. The western shore of India is called the Malabar Coast: the eastern side is the Coromandel Coast.

The climates of India's four regions differ greatly. In the

Typical farm area.

northern mountain and hill country it is cold in the winter, and temperate in the summer. In the North Indian Plain, summers are hot, and there are summer rains. Sometimes there are dust storms. The winters are mild, but sometimes at night it is quite cold. The Deccan is dry except during the monsoon, the period from June to September when the rainy season comes. Along the coast, especially in the coastal plains, the rainfall is very heavy, decreasing with the distance inland. There are parts of India, especially in the west and northwest where annual rainfall is less than eight inches (200 millimeters). This means that the land there is always very dry—much like the deserts of North Africa. Even in the Deccan there is so little rainfall, except during the monsoons, that the rivers often run dry. But along the southeast coast of India and in Assam in the northeast, rainfall may total 400 inches (ten meters) a year.

About 10 percent of India is covered with trees. In the mountainous and hilly areas, there are great expanses of forest

A camel market in one of the desert areas of India.

A view of the Himalayan foothills from Simla.

and jungle. There are also jungles in the Western and Eastern Ghats, and in areas along the southeast and southwest coasts. India's area is about one-third that of the United States. Yet India has over three times as many people as the United States.

India is a mixture of peoples. In the south there are the very dark-skinned people known as the Dravidians. In the extreme east and along the northern borders there are hill people who are related to the races of Burma and Tibet. Living in the jungles of the south and west of India are 25 million people of many tribes: some of them are of mixed Malay and Mongolian descent. Then, throughout the plain of northern India there are people of Indo-European descent—descendants of the Aryans. We will read later how these Aryans came to India many centuries ago. In the mountain valleys of the northwest there are

21

A father-and-son snake-charming team.

people who are blond or partially blond, in contrast with the coloring normally associated with Indians.

Indians call their country *Bharat*. The name India comes from *Sindhu*, the Indian name for the Indus River. From Sindhu come the words Hind, Hindu (man of Hind), Hindustan, Ind and India.

In a country with so much variety in geography and climate and with so many different peoples, there are many different ways of life. But before we learn about these differences, let's learn something about some of India's neighbors.

In the north, India borders on China and Tibet, which is controlled by China. Along the northern border we also find two small countries, Nepal and Bhutan, mountainous and wild, and inhabited by many different tribes. These are independent nations with close relationships with India.

Nepal can now be reached quite easily by road or by plane. It is an interesting country for several reasons. Its mountain people, known as the Gurkhas, are among the best fighters in the world. For many years Gurkhas have fought in the British army and there are many Gurkha troops in the modern Indian Army. Nepal also is the home of the Sherpas, specially trained mountain climbers who are important members of every mountain-climbing expedition in the Himalayas. With their help, Sir Edmund Hillary conquered Mt. Everest, and Sherpas have helped many European expeditions climb other high mountains in the Himalayas.

Now let's look at the map once again. In the far northwest, a

Women of Nepal.

corner of India extends to the Kunlun Mountains of China. This northwest section is called Kashmir, a beautiful area of waterways, mountains and lovely valleys. It is also an area of trouble and dispute, for although Kashmir is claimed and partly occupied by India, it has also been claimed and partly occupied by Pakistan. This is only one of the arguments between these two neighboring countries which until recently were one country. We will learn more about these problems later.

If you look at the map again, you will see that in the east, India really has two different borders. There is a long border with Bangladesh, then a narrow corridor of Indian territory separating

24

Nepal, Tibet, and Bhutan from Bangladesh. This corridor broadens out into a large area of India known as Assam, which joins with Burma to the east and with China to the north. Thus the eastern part of India is almost cut off from the rest of the country. It can be reached only by the narrow corridor that separates Bangladesh from Nepal and Bhutan. It looks as though the borders have been drawn to makes things difficult. In fact, there is no place in the world where the borders seem to make less sense than those between India and her neighbors.

From 1947 until 1970, India was bordered by Pakistan on the east and on the west, but then, after much bloodshed East Pakistan became the independent state of Bangladesh. It is important for us to know why this happened, and why there were

A man from Mysore.

Village life is often simple. Many of its features—such as this water-jar—are the traditional ones which have been known in India through the ages.

two halves to Pakistan, separated by nearly 1,000 miles (1,609 kilometers) of India. So instead of beginning our visit with an account of India's history long ago, we will start with the period when the countries that are now India, Pakistan and Bangladesh were one country governed by Britain. Then we shall ask how it was possible for Britain to control so large an area with so many people for so many years. The answer goes back into the ancient history of the Indian subcontinent and particularly to the religions that were followed by its people.

3

India as a British Colony

In September, 1499, Vasco da Gama arrived back in Portugal after a voyage of many months during which his fleet had visited Calicut, on the Malabar Coast of India. The cargo which da Gama had picked up in Calicut excited the people of Europe, and was to change the way of life of millions of people in Asia.

Vasco da Gama's magic cargo was spices—pepper, nutmeg, cloves. For the most part, the spices were not grown in India, for Calicut was at that time a great trading center for Arab and Indian merchants who imported spices from the Molucca Islands, a part of modern Indonesia. These islands became known to Europeans as the Spice Islands.

At first, the trade in spices was the most important reason for European interest in the East. Wars were fought because of pepper and other spices. The New World was actually discovered when explorers were traveling in search of these spices! Later, however, they lost some of their importance as trade in other goods—such as cloth and precious minerals—began to grow. When European countries took control of India and large parts of Southeast Asia, they did it to protect and extend their own profitable trading activities.

Since early times, there had been some trade between Asia and Europe; but the two continents were separated by deserts and mountains, and by the powerful Ottoman Empire which was Muslim in religion and not on friendly terms with Christian Europe. It was not until the seafaring people of Western Europe built larger ships and dared to believe that the world was not flat that they began to explore far and wide. Even so, the journey from Europe to India and Southeast Asia was long and dangerous. Ships sailed down the coast of Africa, around the Cape of Good Hope and into the Indian Ocean. The round trip might require several years; often ships disappeared and were never heard of again.

The early Portuguese explorers found other exciting products in the East, including beautiful fabrics and gems. But it was the pepper and other spices that had most to do with exploring Asia. Europeans, most of whom were used only to salt and vinegar, were excited at what spice could do to make food more palatable.

Within a few years of Vasco da Gama visiting India, many Portuguese ships were sailing into the Indian Ocean. These ships were large and well-armed, and the resistance of the Arabs who controlled the Indian Ocean was quickly overcome. A famous Portuguese sea captain, Alphonso de Albuquerque, established the first European settlement at Goa on India's west coast in 1505.

For almost a century Portugal controlled the spice trade, and a number of Portuguese trading posts were established in India, in Malaya and in the Spice Islands. But the Dutch, who were expert

India is now a land of great changes, where people are learning new ways. These Delhi schoolgirls, for example, study as hard as their brothers although at one time Indian girls did not attend school.

seamen and shrewd merchants, wasted no time in challenging Portugal's monopoly. Many Dutch expeditions sailed round Africa and into the Indian Ocean so that by the year 1600 there were several Dutch trading posts in India. The Dutch eventually pushed the Portuguese out of the spice trade. Portugal now has nothing of the great area it once controlled. Its last colony—Goa—was occupied by India in 1961.

Soon after the Dutch gained control of the spice trade, they raised the price of pepper. Having a monopoly in the pepper trade meant that they could set any price they wished. In 1587, English merchants had been very much excited when Sir Francis Drake captured a Portuguese ship filled with spices. The cargo was sold for a fabulous sum in England!

So it was that English merchants decided to form a company to trade in spices, and in 1600 the British East India Company was established. Soon company expeditions were sailing to India and the Spice Islands, but they found the Dutch well established, and for some years Dutch and English ships were fierce rivals for the spice trade. In fact, the Dutch control of the Spice Islands made it so difficult to establish trading posts that the British turned to the mainland of Asia, to see what resources they might find there.

For a number of years, the British were too busy fighting the Portuguese to establish many trading posts. Then at last the Portuguese navy was defeated—in 1612 and again in 1614—and the Dutch became too involved in their affairs in the islands of Indonesia to compete with the British in India.

The first British settlement, called St. George, was established in 1639. This tiny fort was to become one of India's greatest ports, and is now called Madras. In 1661, the British also gained control of Bombay, on India's west coast. Bombay (now Mumbai) is now India's second largest city and a great seaport. In 1690, a trading-post was established at Calcutta on the Hooghly River. Calcutta was then only a village; it is now a city of 12,000,000 people.

The history of Europeans in India follows the pattern of their rivalry across the world. England and Holland carried their battles on the mainland of Europe to both America and the East. England prevailed in America and India, while the Dutch established themselves in Indonesia. But other powers, who were less successful, had to be content with much less influential and powerful positions in the East; Portugal was one of these.

India then had its own powerful rulers—the Moguls, descended from Turks who had invaded the country in 1525 and gradually taken control of it. But they began to lose power after 1707 when the Mogul emperor Aurangzeb died. His successors allowed the country to become divided into many independent kingdoms, some of them large, others very small. This lack of unity weakened India, and the British East India Company began to gain control. Between 1746 and 1761, its army defeated several Indian armies and also the French, who had become quite powerful in India. They had established trading centers, and were trying to drive the British out. Even when this French threat was over, the British had many more years of resistance from Indians before they gained control of almost all of what is now India, Pakistan and Bangladesh. From 1814 until 1818, they fought the Gurkhas in northern India. In 1840, they also

31

subdued the people known as Sikhs who, like the Ghurkhas, are fierce Indian warriors.

But although much fighting took place the British often preferred to make arrangements with the rulers of the many independent Indian states, rather than to fight them. The heads of these states, rajahs and sultans, were allowed to keep much of their power in return for favors they granted to the British.

After the Sikhs were defeated, all India came under the rule of the East India Company. It is important to know that it was a business company, rather than the British government, which conquered and began to rule India. The East India Company had become so powerful that in 1852 it also conquered a valuable part of Burma. We might say that the company was a partner of the British government but the soldiers in this partnership were paid by the company rather than by the government.

Unfortunately, there were some unscrupulous and self-seeking men in the East India Company, and many of its officials made

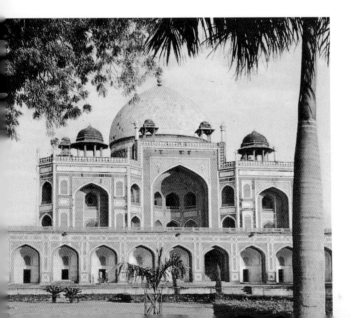

An old Mogul tomb in Delhi.

great fortunes. People in England soon began to feel that the East India Company had too much power. Warren Hastings, one of the early governors, was even brought to trial in England, and the British government tried without success to impeach him for dishonesties in India.

In time, however, the company lost its power and influence. The government of India became more truly a colonial government whose important decisions were made in London. The Governors-General sent from England did many things to create better government in India.

Several social reforms were carried out by the British and some of the cruel customs of Indian society were abolished. One such custom was *suttee* by which it was decreed that a widow must burn herself on the funeral pyre when her husband's body was cremated. There was also a custom which required the drowning of unwanted girl babies. In addition, at that time, slavery still existed in some parts of India. As well as doing away with these customs, the British rulers built new roads and harbors, and several railways. They also established a telegraph system and built schools and colleges which offered an English-style education in India.

Along with these reforms, there was some talk of eventually giving India her independence. The British thought that their rule would prepare the Indians for self-government. Thomas Babington Macaulay, the brilliant nineteenth-century scholar and historian once said, "Whenever it comes, it will be the proudest

A Hindu temple near Calcutta.

day in British history." The day he was speaking of was the day when India became independent.

Yet, for more than a hundred years after Macaulay's declaration, India was to remain subject to Britain. This was the cause of much strife for, while India had welcomed the British as traders, it resented their staying on as rulers. In 1857, Indian resentment led to widespread revolt. The immediate result of this was a mutiny among Indian soldiers who had joined the British army. This mutiny, often called "The Indian Mutiny," soon spread far beyond the army. Much of northern India was in revolt for over a year and many cruel and bloody battles were fought. The Indian forces were led by those princes and rulers who had lost their kingdoms to the British and wanted to win them back. But they failed in their attempts and, by 1858, the British were more strongly established in India than ever before.

The Mutiny marks a very important stage in the story of India. Until it happened the British had governed through the East India Company. But the revolt convinced them that India needed a different form of government. Responsibility for the government of India was taken over by the British Crown in 1858. India became a British colony—the largest and most splendid of Britain's imperial possessions.

Another important effect of the revolt was that, with their defeat, the Indian princes lost all their power. The next challenge to British rule was to come from very different people. These were the people who wished to set up a modern

35

A school which was established by the British and is still run on British public school lines.

and free society in India. Unlike the princes, they had no wish to revert to ancient ways.

There was no strong call for an end to British rule for more than a generation. This, meanwhile, was the heyday of the British in India. They were the most prosperous and scientifically advanced people in the world. They brought to India many of their finest talents—for India was the "jewel in the Empire's crown." The British gave India a strong and stable administration. Commerce and trade were extended and the country benefited in a thousand ways. In 1877, Britain's Queen Victoria was declared "Empress of India." Her subjects thought it their right and responsibility to govern the so-called "backward peoples."

It became fashionable for the sons of fine British families to spend some time in the India Service, or in the British army in India. Many British people spent their whole lives in India. Sometimes life was luxurious for them. Servants were readily available for domestic chores and, in the hot weather, British wives went to the "hill stations" which were summer resorts in the Himalayan foothills. These are still very popular.

British rule did much for India. Roads and railways were built. Among the great cities that were established is New Delhi, built next to old Delhi, the capital city of the Mogul Empire. The British brought peace and a settled administration to large parts of India which had suffered years of turmoil. Uniform law was

A view of Simla, one of the British hill stations.

A British-built canal. By building dams and canals the British brought water to many dry parts of India.

established and many cruel customs were abolished.

But though British rule brought many benefits to India, it was largely for the greater advantage of Britain herself. Indians soon came to demand a greater share in the running of their country. We shall read more of their fight for independence in a later chapter.

Now let's learn about India's ancient history and about the numerous conquerors who came into the North Indian Plain. These conquerors brought different religions with them, and in time religion became a great divider of the people. But India's long history is still glorious, and is filled with romance, fascination and accomplishment.

4

The First Invaders

Archaeologists are scientists who study the life and activities of ancient peoples. Often they try to answer the questions, "Who lived here first, and when? How did they live?" In 1921, archaeologists discovered the remains of a mysterious civilization in the valley of the Indus River. The Indus is the big river which flows from the mountains on India's northwest frontier through present-day Pakistan and into the Arabian Sea.

The Indus Valley peoples built big and well-planned cities almost 5,000 years ago. But these ancient cities are in the part of the Indus Valley which now is in modern Pakistan, so we will consider them as being the earliest known peoples who lived in Pakistan. Who then were the first peoples of India?

We have learned that there are many different peoples living in India, representing four of the five major branches of the human family. Thousands of years ago the most numerous people in India were probably the dark-skinned Dravidians. We do not know very much about the life of the Dravidians. As a matter of fact, the important period of India's past began when invaders came to push the Dravidians from the North Indian Plain.

About 2000 B.C. the first of many invaders pushed through the mountain passes from Central Asia. These people were vigorous nomads. They were fair-skinned and related to the ancient Greeks and Persians. We call these first invaders Indo-Aryans. They pushed into present-day Pakistan and into the North Indian Plain. The Dravidian people, who were no match for them, retreated steadily into southern India.

The invasions from Central Asia continued for over a thousand years until the newcomers had spread throughout the North Indian Plain from the Arabian Sea to the valley of the Ganges River. They built cities, and began to trade throughout the Indian peninsula.

Our knowledge of this long period of conquest and settlement comes from the ancient scriptural books called Vedas. The word *veda* means wisdom. For centuries before they were written down, the accounts of Aryan conquest passed from generation to generation by word of mouth. There are four Vedas which tell us the story of these long-ago days in India, much as the Bible tells us the ancient history of the Jewish people.

But there were more invaders to come before the Indo-Aryan people established themselves firmly in India. Six hundred years before Christ, Persian armies conquered much of India. In the fourth century, Alexander the Great also invaded India and conquered its northern parts. After his death in 323 B.C. one of his generals ruled this area. Then a young warrior named Chandragupta Maurya drove the Greeks from India and established a great Indian empire. We call this the Maurya Dynasty.

Seventh-century rock-carving in Madras.

A grandson of the dynasty's founder, Asoka, became the most famous ruler of this period. The flag of modern India includes the many-spoked "wheel of Asoka." Asoka was a great warrior during the early years of his reign, but he came to hate bloodshed, and even discontinued the royal hunts and forbade the killing of animals for the royal table.

Asoka, who was a Buddhist, built many memorials to Buddhist saints. These were called *stupas*. One of Asoka's capital cities was located at Sarnath, and huge stone pillars fifty feet (over fifteen meters) high still remain from this period, over 2,200 years.

41

In 232 B.C., Asoka died, and soon the Maurya Empire began to fall apart. New invasions came from Central Asia, including tribes known as the Scythians and the Kushans. For over a thousand years after this, India's history was one of wars, invasions, and the rise and fall of small kingdoms.

There was a short period, from A.D. 320 to A.D. 480, when the Gupta Emperors united all of northern India. Under the Guptas, India was prosperous and peaceful. A great university was established, and it attracted students from all over Asia. It was during the Gupta Dynasty that the so-called Arabic system of numbering, which we use today, was invented. Hindu mathematicians developed the system of numbering from 1, 2, 3 to 10. The Persians borrowed the system from the Hindus, and the Arabs borrowed it from the Persians. The last borrower seems to have gained the most credit, for today we call this the Arabic system of numbering!

This camel is raising water by means of a "Persian Wheel," an ancient method still in use in modern India.

The age of the Guptas is known as the Golden Age of Indian art and architecture. During this period the country was prosperous and much labor was used to build splendid monuments. The sculpture of the time reached a new level of excellence. Much progress was also made in the sciences and Indian medicine won fame in many lands. India had developed a highly civilized society. The prosperity of the country came mainly from the produce of the fertile plains of northern India. Unfortunately, it always tempted invaders from the harsher lands to the north and west.

The Gupta Empire lasted less than two hundred years before it collapsed when new invaders called Huns came into India. Again the country experienced what had happened throughout its history. There were many small kingdoms, some lasting for years, others for only a short period.

Unlike China, India had few lengthy periods of strength and greatness. We have not space to mention all the dynasties and kingdoms, some of which existed among the Dravidian and Tamil peoples in the south.

Among the last of the long line of invaders were the Muslims who came to India during the Middle Ages. We shall learn more about them and their impact on India in a later chapter. The last invasion of all was to come from the sea—these invaders were the Europeans about whom we have already read.

However, in spite of many conquerors and long periods of war, the Indian way of life developed during these centuries. This way of life and its religion have been very important, and we must learn something about them in order to understand more about India.

We have used the word Hindu in describing the Gupta mathematicians who invented the system of numbering we use to this day. Now let's learn what Hindu and Hinduism mean, and what effect Hinduism has had on India.

The Aryan invaders who poured into the North Indian Plain over the centuries developed a written language called Sanskrit which is the basis for most of India's modern languages. In time, the sacred Vedas, or Books of Wisdom, were written down in Sanskrit. Other great poems and books were written, developing the ideas of Hinduism that have had such a strong influence on Indian culture. The *Mahabharata* is the longest poem ever written, in 100,000 couplets and 700,000 words. Another great epic poem beloved of Indians is the *Ramayana*. This great Hindu literature telling the story of wars and wanderings also follows the growth of the religious beliefs and system of thought that we call Hinduism. What are the main beliefs of Hindus?

The Hindus believe in a supreme creator who is called Brahma. There are many other gods including Vishnu (the preserver) and Siva (the destroyer). Hindus believe that life is marred by evil, and that the main objective of living is to become free of this evil. The only way the human soul can escape evil is to be reborn again and again, so that the evil is refined out little by little as each life is lived. A person may be reborn many times before the highest and purest state is reached.

Hindu society is organized according to a caste system. This

Plowing in southern India, near Bangalore.

probably began when the Aryans conquered the dark-skinned Dravidians. The tall, fair-skinned Aryans looked down on the Dravidians who did not share their religion. As a result, the Dravidians were given a lower status. Gradually, however, a much more elaborate system was built up.

Caste divides all people into groups according to birth and occupation. At the top are *Brahmans*, the priestly class. This word comes from the word for the supreme god—Brahma.

Beneath them are hundreds of castes. All of them, including the Brahmans, fall into four main divisions. They are the *Kshatriyas*, or warriors; the *Vaisyas*, who were farmers and merchants; and the *Sudras*, who were the serfs. Beneath the four castes come the casteless people sometimes known as the *Untouchables*.

We can see from this that the original divisions of Hindu society according to the caste system were not unlike the classes which existed in medieval Europe.

As society became more complicated and people learned new skills, the castes began to divide into sub-castes. Originally, birth and occupation were the two factors which decided a man's caste. With the growth of new occupations, new factors assumed importance. For example, as gold jewelry gained popularity, a caste of goldsmiths grew up. Similarly, the bakers, confectioners and money-lenders, and people in countless other trades, each had their own groupings.

Up to a point, the caste system was nothing more than a way of dividing labor among the community, like the guilds of

46

An Indian village.

Europe. But after a while the caste rules became more rigid. A person could marry only within his caste. He could only have social relations with members of his own caste. In addition, rules were laid down for eating and drinking. A man could not accept food from a member of a lower caste. Worst of all, the so-called Untouchables led a painful life for they were denied all common privileges.

Modern India has done much to correct the evils of the caste system as they finally developed. The idea of untouchability is now forbidden by law. Those people who suffered from it in the past are now given special privileges in compensation. Much of the good work is the result of the efforts of Mahatma Gandhi, the great Indian leader of modern times, for he always fought for the underprivileged. Even so, much remains to be done before the evils of the system are finally removed.

The caste system is only a part of Hinduism. This religion is distinguished by the depth and splendor of its thought. The *Vedas*, or ancient Aryan hymns, are among the most significant religious texts of the world. The *Gita* is the most beloved of

47

religious books among the Hindus. It has fascinated scholars and ordinary people in many parts of the world.

The Vedas say that the cow is sacred, and a good Hindu cannot kill one. There are nearly 200,000,000 cattle in India, or about thirty cows to every hundred people, and cows wander about everywhere, even in the biggest cities.

Among other important religious groups are India's eighteen million Sikhs. The Sikh religion was founded by Guru (which means Great Teacher) Nanak in the fifteenth century. Sikhs are not divided into castes and they worship one god rather than many gods. A Sikh man will never cut his hair or his beard. The hair is tied up under a beautiful turban, and the beard is sometimes skillfully braided. All Sikh men wear a special bracelet on the wrist, much as Catholics wear little crosses, and they carry a small knife. In olden days Sikhs wore swords rather than small knives, for they were famous fighters. They once led a revolt against the British; but after their defeat, many joined the British army where they distinguished themselves by their warlike qualities. Today this warrior sect provides a large number of the troops of the Indian army. They are also skilled and hard-working farmers in their native province of Punjab.

Jainism is another Indian religion that developed from Hinduism. It was established about 600 B.C. by Mahavira Jnatiputra. Jains have even more respect for the lives of animals than do other Hindus. They will not kill any living thing, and do not believe in violence of any kind. As we shall learn later, the Jain idea of Ahimsa, or preservation of life, was used in

48

A Sikh worshipper standing in front of the Golden Temple at Amritsar.

India's struggle for independence from British rule.

There are about 100,000 followers of the Parsi (or Parsee) religion in India. Fire is sacred to the Parsi whose religion was founded by Zoroaster in Persia about 1000 B.C. A Parsi, because of his worship of fire, will not smoke or pour water on fire. A Parsi must bathe before he prays, and he must pray every morning and every night. When a Parsi dies, the body is placed within what is called a Tower of Silence, and left to be picked clean by vultures, which are large flesh-eating birds. Most Hindus are cremated after death, but this would be a misuse of fire for a Parsi. The Parsi community is small in numbers because no one may become a convert; only a descendent of a Parsi may be a Parsi. But Parsis became important to India because they quickly accepted Western ways. They became teachers, scientists, and excellent businessmen. India's greatest modern steel company was founded by and is operated by a Parsi.

There are about twenty-two million Christians in India, making Christianity India's third largest religion. According to legend, St. Thomas journeyed to the Malabar Coast, and as a result of his preaching, a thriving Christian community developed in the second century. These people, living in the state of Kerala, call their church the Syrian Christian Church. Many Indians were converted after the Europeans came to India. The influence of both Portugal and England resulted in the growth of the Christian community in the country.

Now we come to another great religion, established in India, but with few present-day Indian followers. About the same time as the Jain religion was founded, there were numerous Indians

Pumping water for rice fields; another ancient method.

who were opposed to the caste system, and especially to the power of the Brahmans. They were also critical of the power of the many priests and of the complicated ceremonies of the Hindu religion. Among those opposed to these things was a man named Gautama Siddhartha who came to be called the *Buddha,* or Enlightened One.

Although he was born a nobleman, Buddha was opposed to caste, although he believed in reincarnation or man's rebirth. He also believed that life was evil but that one escaped this evil by good deeds, pure thoughts, and by giving up worldly desires. The emphasis was on a conscious effort by each individual to avoid all violence contributing to the sum of evil in the word.

Buddha lived for eighty years, and gave up his own life to preach his beliefs, wandering through India as a humble monk. We have already read that the Emperor Asoka became a Buddhist. At one time Buddhism was the leading religion of India. Although there are now almost seven million Buddhists in India, Buddhism has become the religion of over 500 million people elsewhere in Asia.

This is a good time for us to realize how much influence India has had on the rest of Asia. Even before Buddhism crossed into China, some Indians were taking either Buddha's message or Hinduism and its sacred books, together with the Sanskrit language, to Southeast Asia. Nearly 2,000 years ago, Indian colonists were sailing across the ocean to the Malay Peninsula, to Indochina, and to the islands of Indonesia. India's lasting

A Rajput veteran. The Rajputs are members of the soldier caste and claim descent from the Kshatriyas.

influence on these countries of Asia has been mainly cultural. Long after the original colonists were absorbed into their new countries, or had returned to India, their customs and religion prevailed.

5

Sons of the Prophet

In the year A.D. 711, Arabs had begun to settle around the mouth of the Indus River in what is now Pakistan. These Arabs were followers of the Muslim religion. They conquered territory in the valleys of the Indus, but for over two centuries they did not have much effect upon India.

Then in A.D. 998, a Muslim army led by the Amir Mahmud of Ghazni began to raid Indian territory from Afghanistan. The Hindus fought bravely against the new invaders, but they were no match for the Muslim warriors, who used swift Arab war horses against the slow Indian war elephants. There were many other reasons for the success of the invaders. One was that their opponents were divided among themselves and incapable of coming together. In addition, the caste system weakened them, for only one section of the population—the warrior class—was supposed to fight.

These new invaders brought with them a religion which became the greatest divider of all. In fact, it not only divided people, but in time created two independent nations. It was this religious division that led to the strange geographical partition of the Indian

The Rajput fortress of Amber near Jaipur. The Rajputs, a warrior caste, fought the Muslims for many years.

subcontinent when the British finally withdrew.

For many years, the Muslims continued to raid and occupy Indian territory. Finally in A.D. 1191, a powerful Muslim named Mohammed Ghori began to raid, and gradually occupied large parts of India. For the next five hundred years, most of the country was under Muslim rule, and in 1526 the Muslim Mogul Dynasty was founded. This became the most powerful dynasty in India's history.

The religion of India's new rulers was founded by Mohammed, who was born in Arabia in the sixth century A.D. Believers in this religion are also called Mohammedans, and the religion is sometimes known as Islam. The teachings of Mohammed the Prophet are written down in a sacred book called the Koran. These beliefs are totally different from the beliefs of the Hindus. Muslims believe in one God, and they hold that all people are created equal. The idea of caste was so strange to the Muslims that they could not accept it, nor could they understand the Hindus having many gods.

Already divided into many small states, India was at first divided even further by the powerful new religion which gained many converts in the course of time. But soon the Muslims began to rule as Indians rather than as foreign conquerors. The Mogul Emperor, Akbar the Great, went so far as to try to develop a new religion which would unite his subjects. Just as the Aryans had entered India as invaders, and then settled down as people of the country, so the Muslims, too, made India their home.

Unfortunately, their religion remained an obstacle to the unity of the people of India as a whole. Some Mogul rulers, unlike Akbar, treated Hindus badly. They were made to pay special taxes and were persecuted in many other ways. The result was that these religious and social differences persisted for centuries.

The Moguls were great builders as well as good fighters, and some of India's most famous buildings were erected by Mogul emperors, or shahs. The world-famous Taj Mahal at Agra is often called the most beautiful building on earth. It was built by the Shah Jahan as a memorial to his favorite wife when she died young.

During the centuries of Muslim raids and rule, many more

The Taj Mahal, one of the world's most beautiful buildings.

Muslims came into India, while many Indians became Muslims. The people living in the valley of the Indus River became Muslim in great numbers. This is the area closest to the mountain passes through which the Muslim invaders came. It is also close to the Arabian Peninsula from which other Muslims came by sea.

In some parts of India, there were not many converts to the new religion. However, in the extreme eastern part, around the mouth of the Ganges River, most of the people became Muslims. Altogether, by the time Great Britain gained control of the Indian subcontinent, about one out of every four people was a follower of Mohammed.

So great was the division caused by religion that, when the country finally gained independence, the Muslims demanded and obtained a separate State. This resulted in the curious boundaries of India and Pakistan, since it was the two areas which became East and West Pakistan which had the largest Muslim communities. There are, however, over 105 million Muslims in India. Today India is a State without an official religion. Her citizens include people of many different religions.

Although it existed in name for many years, the Mogul Empire began to fall apart in 1707. There were many revolts against the Moguls; and, as happened so frequently in India's history, numerous small independent kingdoms were established. There were independent Hindu states and independent Muslim states so that India became more divided than ever. It was during this period after 1707 that the British East India Company began to gain control of India. By the

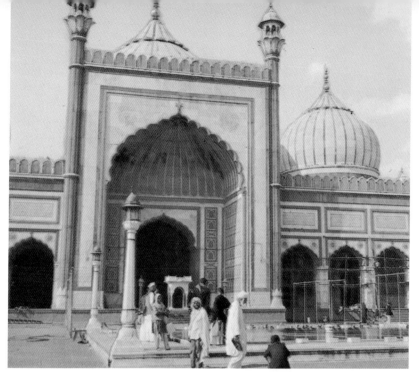

The principal mosque in Delhi.

middle of the nineteenth century, this control was complete.

Now that we have read about India's history and of the reasons why it was easy for Great Britain to control so populous a land, let's learn how independence was finally achieved.

Many countries of the world have won their freedom after years of hard military struggles. In sharp contrast, *no* armies, *no* generals were involved in India's fight for freedom. India's independence was achieved mainly by following non-violent methods, an adaptation of the ancient Jain idea of *Ahimsa*.

6

The Struggle for Independence

As we have seen, at the end of the period of Mogul rule, the country had been split up into a number of small states which were often hostile to each other. This made it possible for the British to gain a foothold in India and gradually extend their rule over the entire country. The Indians could not match the advances already made by Britain in the Industrial Revolution. Nevertheless, they had a constant desire, even at this time, to regain freedom. This took the form of the armed revolt of 1857 about which we read earlier.

Some time later, however, the call for independence was renewed in a fresh form. Instead of weapons, the new leaders were armed with ideas. As communications improved and as the effect of the English schools began to be felt, Indians came into contact with modern European thought. Their demand for greater privileges had its parallel in the advances made by the common people in the more powerful countries of Europe. Perhaps the most important reason for this was the spread of education in the English language.

There are cowboys in India too! These Indian boys are learning how to breed and raise healthier cattle.

Many English schools were set up by missionaries, and often their pupils went on to study at universities established by the government.

A few Indians went to England to study. Educated Indians began urging their countrymen to learn about the rest of the world, to become educated and learn new ways. Indian leaders also began a Hindu revival. This means that they urged their people to remember the glories of the past and to learn more about the accomplishments of their great kings so that they might gain a sense of national future.

In 1885, a number of educated Indians formed an organization called the Indian National Congress, which met at Poona, near Mumbai (Bombay). Only seventy people attended the first meeting, and of these only two were Muslims. The National Congress was not at first a political group. It met in a different city each year, and its leaders were mainly interested in social reform. Some members urged the British to start compulsory education; others were interested in projects to help the millions of Untouchables and other low-caste people.

However, each year there was more discussion of self-government, more criticism of British rule and more demand for change. Those leaders who wanted moderate reforms were ousted by others who called for complete independence. In 1907, the great Indian patriot Tilak thrilled his fellow-countrymen with the words: "*Swaraj* (self-government) is my birthright and I will have it." By the time the First World War began, in 1914, the leaders of the Indian National Congress were all echoing Tilak's cry.

We must understand that most of the Indian leaders had no hatred for the British. In the war, Indians fought alongside British troops. Nor did they wish to turn their backs on all that the British had achieved in India. They appreciated what progress had been made—but, of course, they were also very well aware of the obligations imposed upon them by foreign rule. Their united call was for total independence.

India's struggle for independence continued for many years, and among its leaders we have space to mention only three men. Mohandas Gandhi became the best known and India's greatest hero. The other two were father and son, Motilal and Jawaharlal Nehru. Motilal, the father, was a wealthy lawyer who became one of Gandhi's most active supporters. Jawaharlal became India's first prime minister and one of the world's best-known statesmen.

Gandhi was born in 1869 near Mumbai (Bombay). He came from an orthodox Hindu family who observed their traditional religious customs. Because young Gandhi wanted to be a lawyer, he went to England to study. In his autobiography, he describes how he almost starved until he discovered a vegetarian restaurant! In 1891, Gandhi returned to India, and two years later he went to South Africa to take up legal practice.

Gandhi became a successful and prosperous lawyer. He also became interested in the problems of the many Indians living in South Africa. The Indians there suffered great discrimination from the European residents and from the government. The young lawyer took up his countrymen's fight for better working conditions, for more rights and for an end to discrimination.

The former British Viceroy's House lit for the festival of Divali.

We have read about Ahimsa, the idea of preservation of life or non-violence, advocated by the religious teacher who founded Jainism in the sixth century. Gandhi began to study and to use Ahimsa. Under his leadership, thousands of Indians in South Africa simply sat down on their jobs or went on hunger strikes. They accepted arrest and would never fight back. The courage of the Indians aroused public opinion in England and in India, and the South African government eventually made many of the changes demanded by Gandhi

When Gandhi returned to India, after a visit to England, he was a public hero. He became known as the Mahatma. which means the Great Soul. It is interesting that on his visit to England, which took place in 1914 just as England went to war, Gandhi urged all Indians to support the British war effort.

In India, Gandhi established an *ashram* or school, and many

Indians came to hear him teach. He believed that India could win its freedom through *Ahimsa*, or as he said, "by sympathy, patience, and long-suffering." Within a few years, Gandhi had an opportunity to try non-violence on a national scale.

In 1919, the British government passed a number of laws to help control terrorism in India. There had been cases of Indians bombing trains, or shooting British soldiers from ambush. The new laws, called the Rowlatt Acts, gave the government power to arrest and judge people without trial, or to put suspected terrorists in prison without trial. Indian leaders were opposed to these laws. They said that they were undemocratic and gave the government

Like this one, many roads throughout India are still unpaved.

far too much power. Gandhi appealed to his countrymen to observe a *hartal*, or day of prayer, in opposition. Everyone was urged to stop work, to close shops and to fast.

Unfortunately, the non-violent approach of the Indians was not able to last out to the end. There were riots, soldiers were called in to restore order, and they fired into the crowds. Gandhi was arrested, and although he was released in a few days, the news of his arrest caused more riots.

In the city of Amritsar, the Sikh city near Lahore, the rioting became serious. A British general who arrived with some soldiers foolishly ordered his men to fire again and again into a great crowd of people. The people were merely listening to speeches, and the firing began without warning. Nearly 1,500 men, women and children were killed or injured.

The news of the Amritsar massacre spread and caused great agitation throughout the country. This was the turning point of the independence movement. The Indians who had formerly not been involved in it were now shocked into the realization that their foreign rulers must go.

In 1921, Mahatma Gandhi led a nation-wide non-co-operation movement. The Indians hoped that by not paying taxes or participating in the running of the country in any way, they would make it impossible for the government to function. Students left their schools and colleges, and all kinds of ordinary people prepared themselves to go to jail, if necessary, in defiance of British authority. India had never seen anything like this before. The whole country was united. This unified effort was very successful but it was marred by an act of mob violence which pained Gandhi deeply. He decided that the country was not yet ready for the discipline of non-violence and he called the whole movement off. This was not a popular move, but Gandhi placed principle above all other considerations. For him, the means was as important as the end.

The British government was also shocked by the Amritsar massacre, by the bombings and murders by terrorists. The British were anxious to make changes and to give the people more voice in their government, but they were not prepared to give as much as the Indians demanded. Besides, differences arose among the Indians themselves. For several years, Muslim leaders co-operated with Hindus, and many joined the National Congress. Although there were 100 million Muslims in India, they were not well organized. Muslim leaders became afraid that self-government would leave them without protection from the more numerous and better-organized Hindus. These fears led to the formation of a Muslim political group called the Muslim League. Under the leadership of Mohammed Ali Jinnah, the Muslim League became better organized to fight for conditions that would assure them equality with Hindus.

Perhaps the biggest problem was that British reforms were too slow. The people, whether Muslim or Hindu, wanted independence at once and not in gradual steps. Gandhi began to turn against the British who had arrested and imprisoned him on several occasions. And he began to share leadership with Jawaharlal Nehru who had also been educated in England and had returned to India with many ideas about how to help his people.

In 1930 another movement of defiance took place. The government controlled the salt business and taxed all salt produced or sold. Gandhi selected the salt tax as a symbol of oppression. On March 12th, he began a march to the sea which was far away from his headquarters. When Gandhi and his followers reached the sea, they picked up pinches of natural salt that had dried out from the water. This was to symbolize defiance of the government and the salt tax.

Immediately a new civil disobedience campaign began. This time it was a great success, and the business life of India became paralyzed. Once again, Gandhi was arrested, and 60,000 other members of the Congress with him.

Then, on September 3, 1939, Great Britain declared war on Germany, and the Viceroy of India, representing the British Crown, proclaimed that India also was at war. The Congress Party protested on the grounds that the consent of the people had not been obtained, and Gandhi announced that as a believer in non-violence he could not support the war.

In 1941, the war took a new turn when Japan attacked Pearl Harbor and captured Malaya and Singapore. Japanese armies then occupied Burma, invaded eastern India and bombed Calcutta.

These events divided the Congress. Gandhi wanted all British troops to leave India, and, as he said, "leave India in God's hands." Other leaders wanted to fight against Japan and argue about freedom later. Nehru was willing for India to help Great Britain but only if India were granted immediate independence.

An old woman using the spinning wheel that Gandhi made a national symbol of independence.

The British could not afford to have trouble in India in the middle of a desperate war. The government sent Sir Stafford Cripps, a man who had long advocated independence for India, to work out a solution. After meeting with Muslim and Hindu leaders, Cripps offered India complete independence as a member of the British Commonwealth of Nations. He promised that all British troops would leave; and that the new India could, if it wished, leave the Commonwealth and become completely free. However, he said that these things could not be granted while Great Britain was in a life-and-death struggle with Japan and Germany. In other words, the Indians could have what they wished after the war was won.

Every major Indian political party, including the Muslim League, turned the offer down. Gandhi threatened to declare another nationwide disobedience campaign. Quickly the British government arrested him, along with Nehru and hundreds of other leaders.

After the end of the Second World War, Great Britain had a new government led by the Labour Party whose leaders had always urged Indian independence. The British people had suffered much during the war. They were tired of the squabbling in India. As far as most people in England were concerned, the sooner India was free the better. Therefore Great Britain offered India complete independence. The new nation would be a dominion within the British Commonwealth of Nations, or it could decide to cut all ties with England. A Constituent Assembly would be elected, and this body would be responsible for drafting a constitution.

But differences between Muslim and Hindu leaders had become so great that no constitution could be drafted or government established which would satisfy both groups.

On August 16, 1946, the Muslim leaders called a *hartal,* or day of prayer. They wanted to bring attention to their views on freedom. Terrible riots broke out between Muslims and Hindus. In Calcutta alone, over 5,000 people were killed. The Muslim League leaders can perhaps be blamed for this particular event. On the other hand, Congress leaders, including Nehru, had made statements which frightened the Muslims, who became certain that the Hindus would control the new government.

The idea of partition, or separate Muslim and Hindu countries, had been suggested from time to time. The British were opposed to this idea. The roads, postal and telegraph systems had been

A scene in Kashmir.

planned for one big country. There were some Hindus and some Muslims living in every province or state, and in every independent state. The big state of Kashmir was ruled by a Hindu maharajah, while most of the people were Muslim. Hyderabad was ruled by a Muslim, but the people were Hindus. But, in spite of these problems, division into two separate nations seemed to be the only solution.

We have already learned that most of the people living in the Indus Valley were Muslims, and that there were also many Muslims in eastern India. British, Muslim and Hindu leaders worked together to try to draw boundaries which would create Muslim states in the Indus Valley region and in the part of eastern India along the lower Ganges and Brahmaputra rivers. However, it was impossible not to draw boundaries that would leave millions of Muslims living in India and millions of Hindus living in either part of the proposed new Muslim state, to be called Pakistan. It was decided that the many independent princely states would decide later on whether to be a part of India or a part of Pakistan, or try to remain independent.

In England, the bill granting complete independence was introduced in Parliament on July 4, 1947, and was quickly passed so that at midnight on August 14th, India and Pakistan became free and independent members of the British Commonwealth of Nations. But independence did not solve the Muslim-Hindu problem. It only became worse. Within a few days, riots broke out in many parts of the subcontinent. Muslims attacked Hindus, Hindus attacked Muslims; sometimes Sikhs killed both Muslims and Hindus. Hundreds of villages were burned, and tens of thousands of men, women and children were killed. Thousands of Hindus, finding themselves living in the new Muslim Pakistan, tried to escape. Muslims left living in Indian territory fled toward one of the two sections of Pakistan. Huge caravans, often numbering 50,000 people, travelled on foot, carrying everything they owned. Often the escaping caravans were attacked and burned, and the people murdered or kidnapped. By the end of the year, nearly twelve million people had fled their homes and hundreds of thousands of people had been killed.

For a time, it appeared that nothing could stop the killing of Hindus by Muslims, and of Muslims by Hindus. Then it was that Mahatma Gandhi won a great victory. He made an appeal for a nationwide day of prayer and fasting. Muslims and Hindus alike came to their senses, and for a time there was peace.

However, peace between Hindus and Muslims did not last long. New trouble broke out over the State of Kashmir. Muslims were afraid that the Hindu maharajah would join India. An invasion by tribesmen from Muslim areas in Pakistan sought to settle the issue by removing the ruler by force. The tribesmen defeated the Kashmiri troops and advanced to within a short distance of the capital. The maharajah then joined his State to India and asked for help. This help was given. Indian troops were flown into Kashmir. They saved the capital and engaged in battle with the invaders who now included troops of the Pakistan army.

For a while it appeared that India and Pakistan would go to war. There was a new wave of hatred in both countries. Once again,

Gandhi appealed for reason. On January 13, 1948, he started a fast. He hoped that by starving himself as an example of self-sacrifice, he could persuade other Hindus to overcome their hatred of Muslims. Two weeks later, Gandhi was murdered by a Hindu who believed him to be too soft with the Muslims.

Perhaps in his death Gandhi won his greatest victory; for his murder shocked Muslims and Hindus alike, and made them ashamed. Men of both nations realized that they could not afford to begin killing one another again.

Mahatma Gandhi deserves much of the credit for India's independence. Sometimes his disobedience campaigns did not work; sometimes Ahimsa ended in fighting. But for years Gandhi was a symbol to his people.

But although Gandhi's death averted war between Hindus and

A rural family typical of India's poverty-stricken millions.

Muslims, it did not solve all the problems between India and Pakistan. It did not alter the map of the new India, which was carved up so strangely. The boundaries between India and Pakistan are still based on religion rather than race or language, or natural borders such as rivers or mountains. We will read later about some of the problems caused by these boundaries. Now let's learn about modern India, its government, and how its people live.

7

India Today

Soon after becoming independent and separate from Pakistan, India drafted a constitution and set up a permanent government. Thus India became a republic; she is a member of the British Commonwealth of Nations but is *not* a dominion. This means that relations with Great Britain are not as close as they are in the case of Canada or Australia.

India has a parliament, made up of two houses in some ways like the two houses of the British parliament. The upper house is called the *Rajya Sabha* or Council of States, and has about 245 members. The lower house is called the *Lok Sabha* or House of the People. It has about 545 members. Parliament is the lawmaking body, and its members are elected by the people.

The President of India is elected for five-year terms by the members of Parliament and the members of state legislatures. The Vice President is elected by members of Parliament. The President is not the head of the government. He appoints a Prime Minister who, in turn, selects his cabinet—called the Council of Ministers. In this way, the government of India is very similar to that of Great Britain.

India is divided into twenty-five states and seven territories. The territories include some mountainous frontier areas, islands in the Bay of Bengal, and Delhi. New Delhi, the capital, is not a part of any state but is governed as a part of the Delhi Territory.

Each state has an elected legislature of one or two houses. Each state governor, however, is appointed by the President. This means that in India the central, or federal, government has more power than the state governments.

There are several political parties in India but for many years the Congress Party was more powerful than all the others. We have read about the Indian National Congress that first met in 1885. This organization became the Congress Party and it won control of India's government immediately after independence. Jawaharlal Nehru became its parliamentary leader and India's first prime

India's flag. It has bands of saffron yellow, white and green, and includes a blue wheel of Asoka copied from a carved pillar at Sarnath.

minister. He continued in this office until his death in 1964.

The next prime minister, Lal Bahadur Shastri, died after only two years in office. He was followed by Indira Gandhi, the daughter of Nehru (and not related to Mahatma Gandhi). Under Mrs. Gandhi, the Congress Party grew even more powerful; for a time it could almost be said that India had a one-party government. However, Mrs. Gandhi and her party quickly lost their popularity when they began to act in a way which seemed undemocratic. In the elections of 1977 they were very heavily defeated by a group of parties called the Janata Coalition, but the parties of the coalition soon found that they could not agree and their government collapsed.

Meanwhile, there had also been much disagreement among the members of the Congress Party. This led to the formation of a new party by Mrs. Gandhi's supporters. This party won a large majority in the elections of 1980.

In 1984, Indira Ghandi was assassinated by one of her own bodyguards. Rajiv Gandhi led the nation until his assassination in 1991. In the 1980s and 1990s, the Sikhs were looking to establish an independent state in Punjab; this and other religious and ethnic conflicts surfaced throughout the country.

India's government is quite strong now, in spite of the many difficulties which the nation faced when it became independent. All of the hundreds of independent princely states had to decide whether to become a part of India or of Pakistan or to remain independent. None chose to be independent. The organization of India had to be changed as the princely states joined the nation. New boundaries were drawn. Before the present system of states and territories could be established, there were serious troubles. Most of these troubles were over language and state boundaries. Often there were bloody riots as people speaking the same language objected to new boundaries which did not include all people speaking that language.

India's first election took place in 1952. It was the largest election ever held in history, and took four months. At that time, 83 percent of the people could not read. Each party and independent candidate was given a symbol so that illiterate people would know for whom they were voting. There were altogether 224,000 voting booths. In spite of these difficulties, a large proportion of people voted.

Language still remains one of India's problems. The constitution made Hindi the official language. However, many of the best newspapers and magazines are published in English; English is the language of business, of the courts and also of parliament. It was also an official language of India until 1965; now it is called an associate language used for some government work and in many institutes of higher education. We will learn more about Hindi and the other important languages in the next section.

The Indian constitution guarantees freedom of speech and religion, and abolishes Untouchability. But the caste system which has existed for hundreds of years has not been completely abolished. Laws do not necessarily change people's ways of thinking about race or religion. Caste is still a problem in India.

Indians of different religions have made great progress in

learning to live and work together. However, problems can still arise very easily—as, for instance, in mid-1984 when a political quarrel between some Sikhs and the government led to fighting and much loss of life, and eventually (in October 1984) to the assassination of Indira Gandhi.

Now let's learn what life would be like if you lived in India. What are houses like, what food is eaten, what clothing is worn by the people of modern India?

There is no place in the world where one's daily life depends as much on religion as in India. If you lived in India, even your name might depend on your religion. If your last name were Singh, you almost certainly would be a Sikh. *All* Sikhs are named Singh; but not all people named Singh are Sikhs. If your last name were Khan, you would be from a Muslim family. Also, if you were a boy named Muhammed, Ali, Ahmad, or Husain, you would be a Muslim. Most names ending in "walla," such as Daruwalla, are Parsi. The last names Iyer or Iyengar are common, and always belong to southern Indian Brahman families.

If your family were high-caste Hindu, you would probably eat no meat at all, and no eggs. Lower-caste Hindus eat only mutton, no pork, and especially not beef. Muslims eat mutton, sometimes beef but never pork. Among educated modern Indians in the big cities, these dietary laws are not so important as they once were. There are Indians who eat meat and eggs, who use knives and forks, who live in every way much as we do. However, in this book we want to learn about average people. And among average Indians, living conditions, food, and religious beliefs have not

A village near New Delhi with thatch-roofed houses.

changed very much from the past.

We have been talking about food, so let's first learn about the daily food of an average Indian family. Notice the picture of an Indian man cooking. He is making chapatties, which look like pancakes; they are made from wheat and are baked into thin, unleavened cakes.

For most Indians, chapatties are an important part of every meal. They are eaten with curry made with vegetables and meat. Sometimes, the curry spices have so much red chili pepper that it is terribly "hot" for an American or European, but many Indians like their curry to be much milder than

79

Americans and Europeans imagine.

If you were to sit down to an Indian meal, you would probably sit on the floor. There would be no knives or forks on the low table placed before you. Indians eat with their fingers, and chapatties are very helpful. Instead of having to dip your fingers into the curry stew, you would use pieces of chapatti to pick up each mouthful. Often a big banana leaf is used instead of a plate.

Food is somewhat different in the various parts of India. In southern India, rice is the most important cereal. In northern India, wheat made into chapatties is the most important. In some places, *jawar,* a kind of millet, is the basic food. Jawar is baked into cakes which are thicker and larger than chapatties,

Making chapatties.

A woman of the south drawing water from the village well.

and are called *bhaker*. If your family were well-to-do, there would be more rice and less wheat and jawar in your daily food.

From the pictures in this section, you can see that most Indians live simply. In some parts of India, houses are rectangular and flat-topped. In other parts, the houses have cone-shaped roofs made of thatch. Those in our picture look much like houses we might expect to see in Africa. More of these are seen in southern India.

The average low-income home has very little furniture, and the floors are either of hard-packed mud or dried cow dung.

Many people still use simple implements passed down through the centuries. Below there is a strange picture. The white stuff is homemade noodles. The noodles are hung on the branches of a tree to dry. The woman's face is covered because she is in *purdah*—that is, she will not let her face be seen, except when she is inside her own home. Purdah is a Muslim custom followed by many Hindu women. Muslims believe their women must be very modest, must never mix socially with men, and must

A woman in purdah hangs homemade noodles on tree branches to dry.

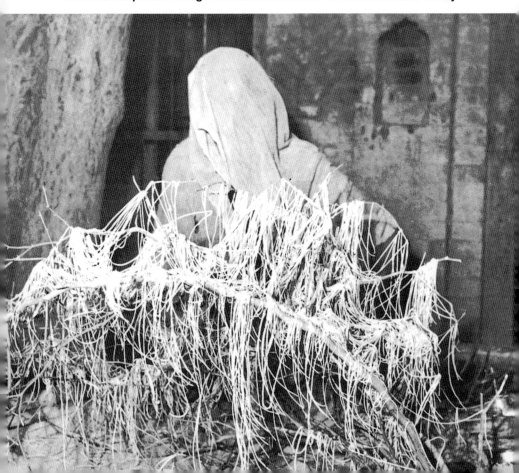

always keep their faces covered when they are outside the home.

The pictures will also give us an idea of Indian clothing. Since it is hot most of the year, clothing is light and loose. Men wear a *dhoti*, a long piece of cotton cloth wrapped around the waist with one piece passed between the legs. This gives the *dhoti* a gathered, baggy look. Many boys wear shorts and, in the hot months, nothing else. Of course, in the big cities many men wear Western-style clothing. Loosely wound turbans are worn by most men instead of hats. Even small boys have turbans. We have read about the fancy turbans worn by Sikhs. Turbans are made in all shades, pale or bright, and are very colorful.

The most popular dress for women is the *sari*, which may be very plain or, among wealthy people, very rich and beautiful. The *sari* is a very long wide piece of cloth which is first of all wound around the woman's waist, with some pleats in front. The remaining length of material is then drawn up across her shoulder or draped gracefully over her head. The exact method of draping a *sari* often differs according to the part of India from which a woman comes. A tight short-sleeved blouse and a floor-length petticoat are worn under the *sari*.

If you lived in India you might not go to school. Education is one of the country's biggest problems. Since independence, the government has built many schools, and free education is now available to all children. However, it is not easy for some children to take advantage of it. And it may be many years before all children can be educated.

An open-air class in a village school.

At present, about one-fifth of the children in India between the ages of six and eleven have no school education.

The picture on page 86 shows an Indian boy named Samsingh. He is on his way to school. In one hand he is carrying some books; in the other hand he has a lantern and a winnowing basket. Samsingh, like many other Indian boys, will go to school during the day; then he must work far into the night, helping a farmer with the rice harvest.

On the facing page there is a picture of a school in action. The Indian government will supply a teacher for any village which will provide a building. You can see that this school building is very crude, but at least the children can study here.

Indian boys and girls study arithmetic, science and history. They begin studying in their own language, but if they go very far in school, they must study English; for English is the chief medium of higher education.

Although the Indian Constitution recognizes eighteen different Indian languages, about 20 percent of the people speak Hindi, which was developed from the Sanskrit of the Aryans who came to India centuries ago. It is strange that the other Sanskrit languages of northern and central India, although written in the same script, often sound quite different from each other when spoken. For instance, "Let's take a trip to India" would sound like this in Hindi: *Ham bharat ser kar aien.* But in Marathi, which is spoken in southwest India, it would be: *Bharatala prawas keru ya.* Furthermore, in southern India, there are four Dravidian

Samsingh is ready for school.

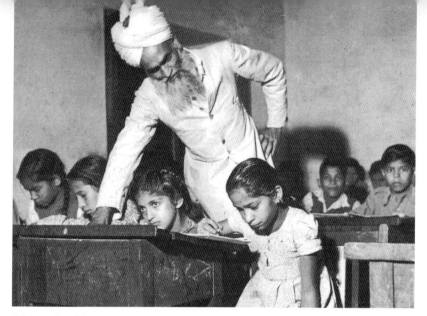

This school has proper classrooms.

languages which are neither written nor spoken like Hindi. Hindi is now the only national language, with English taking second place. All children in India are taught in their local language in the first stages. Later they study both Hindi and English as well.

Now let's see what Hindi looks like. Next to English and Chinese, more people speak Hindi than any other language in the world. There are sixty-one letters in the alphabet. It is a phonetic system of writing. This means that words are written exactly as they sound, which is different from English. In English we must learn that cough is spelled c-o-u-g-h, rather than k-o-f, which is more the way it sounds; but in Hindi every word is written exactly as it sounds.

On this page you can see many of the letters of the Hindi alphabet. It is written from left to right as in English. After the letters of a word are put together, there must be a line on the top, touching the heads of the letters in the word, like this ————. This line is very important because it shows when a word has been completed. Most of the Indian languages are written in this alphabet, called *Devanagari* script. All of the languages which use this script have a certain number of words in common.

There is another language, spoken by quite a few Indians, which uses Persian letters. This language is called Urdu. It is also the most important language of Pakistan. Urdu is written from right to left.

क   ख   ग   घ   ङ

च   छ   ज   झ   ञ

ट   ठ   ड   ढ   ण

त   थ   द   ध   न

ौ –औरत कौवा

ाँ –अंगूर ऊँट आँख

Indian children at a mission school.

Many Indians speak Bengali, the main language of Bangladesh. This means that the people of Bangladesh can talk to their Indian neighbors but not to the Urdu-speaking people of Pakistan who were once their compatriots in the divided Pakistan. Often educated Indians must speak English in order to understand each other.

From what we have read, it seems that Indian boys and girls live hard lives. More than one third of the people are poor; their homes are small; many boys and girls cannot go to school. Outsiders who visit India are often shocked by so much poverty. This is especially so in the big cities, where many people have nowhere to sleep except on the pavements. And all over India, there are holy men, or religious beggars, who are fed by believers. There are about

89

three million of these holy men who live by begging. However, as we have said, India is a land of great contrasts. There are some extremely wealthy people who live in homes which are like palaces. There are many modern-minded families who no longer follow ancient Hindu ways. And even among the poor, there is fun. Let's learn about some of the big festivals of India and of some of the things which Indian boys and girls do for fun.

There are many, many festivals connected with the Hindu religion. *Holi* is the festival celebrating the coming of spring; the festival of *Dussehra* comes at the end of the rains. *Divali*, or the festival of lights, comes at the beginning of winter. During this festival, houses and whole cities are bright with hundreds of lights. There are also fireworks and feasts. Boys and girls like Divali because during this festival there are three weeks of school holidays.

Then there are especially holy places which devout people like to visit. Every year thousands of people go to bathe in the waters of the Ganges, which is India's most holy river. Hindus believe in ritual purification through bathing in a sacred river. The Ganges is called "Mother Ganges," and towns along its banks are visited by tens of thousands of people.

There are many holy places along the Ganges, but the city of Varansi (Benares) is the most important. When Hindus die, they are cremated. Just as it is the wish of all good Muslims to visit Mecca, the Muslim holy city, it is the wish of Hindus that their ashes may be scattered on the Ganges at Haridwar. If you were to visit Haridwar, you might think that there was a great fire; for everywhere along the river bank, smoke rises from the burning ghats. These are stone steps on which the bodies of the dead are placed for cremation. A pilgrimage to Varansi (Benares) or to some other Hindu holy place is serious business for the grown-ups. For the children, however, these trips are exciting and interesting.

On this page, there is a picture which shows another form of fun which Indian boys and girls love. The oxcart is advertising an old American film! However, Indians do not have to rely on American or other imported films. India has its own film industry—a very big one which makes more films than any other country in the world.

8

Farmers and Factories

About 50 percent of India's people are farmers, for India is predominantly an agricultural country. Indian farmers must raise the rice that is the most important food in southern and eastern India, and the wheat that is important in the north. India is the second largest producer of rice in the world.

We might be surprised at some of the other important crops. India is third in the world as a grower of tobacco. India produces more peanuts and tea than any other nation. If your mother has ever given you a dose of castor oil, you probably can thank India; for it is one of the world's leading producers of the castor bean.

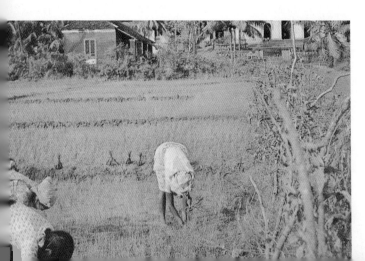

Planting rice in eastern India.

India is also the leading producer of jute, a plant which is grown on the damper areas. Its fiber is used for making canvas, sacking and matting.

Cotton is another important product; the making of cotton and other cloth is India's most important industry. Steel, machinery, chemicals, and computer software are also made in large quantities. India is among the ten biggest industrial countries of the world. Its forested areas produce fine timber, including teak, a very hard wood. Beneath the ground, there are rich deposits of iron ore, coal, manganese, and mica.

A good transportation system is important for farmers and factories alike. India is fortunate in that the British built an excellent system of roads and railways. Since becoming independent, India has added many more roads.

India has excellent air passenger services within the country and also to other parts of the world. The planes of Air-India International fly to Europe, Africa and most of the capital cities of the Far East.

With its planes, trains, and thousands of buses, India also has

Indian farmers are eager to try out new equipment like this tractor.

other less modern ways of travel. Oxcarts and camel carts are common. In many small towns the *tonga* is also used. This is a two-wheeled horse carriage in which the passengers face the rear.

All over India, we see varieties of the rickshaw, or jin-rickshaw. Rickshaws were first used in Japan, and for many years were pulled by a man who ran between two long shafts. There are no longer any rickshaws in Japan, and in other parts of Asia the rickshaw has been changed to become a pedicab. In this, a bicycle is fastened between the shafts so that instead of trotting, the pedicab man pedals. Old-style rickshaws are still used in Calcutta, Madras and other cities of southern India. Pedicabs have taken their place in Mumbai (Bombay) and Delhi. In other cities, three-wheeled motor scooters are now used instead of pedicabs or rickshaws.

Now we will read about India's problems and what she is doing to overcome them.

One of the many buses on India's highways.

9

India's Problems

India's chief problems are poverty and the religious diversions within the country. Vast numbers of people have to survive on too little food and live in unsatisfactory dwellings. The result is malnutrition and disease. As the population keeps increasing, the little that there is has to provide for more people. Since 1992 economic reforms have been made and the economy is expanding. India is reaching out to attract the multinational economic powers. Food production is steadily rising with increases in irrigation and the use of fertilizers and pesticides.

Vital services like schools need to be addressed and the literacy rate of 54 percent improved. The country is aiming at a fairer distribution of money among all its people. Even more important than giving each person what he or she requires is to provide for the people as a whole those things that are necessary for their well-being, including schools, hospitals and roads.

Skyscraper apartments in Mumbai (Bombay).

The religious divisions of the country take their toll. These divisions cause rioting to break out frequently and tensions to rise constantly.

The train system in India has been going through a modernization period and India has the fourth-largest rail system in the world. India is trying to meet the needs of an expanding industrial center. The country has been very successful in its industrial development. In many places newly-completed projects are helping to create the wealth without which no progress can be made.

One result of the growth of industry has been the lessening of caste distinctions between people. We saw earlier how individuals were separated from each other by the caste system. As one caste often did only one kind of work, it gave its

96

members a chance to live more or less apart from others. But a big factory employs thousands of workers from many different backgrounds. They all have to live and work together, and gradually the differences in their castes come to count for very little. In this, and many other ways, a new society is developing in India. People are beginning to be free of the attitudes that bound them for centuries.

India has always wanted peace throughout the world, for without peace there can be no progress. In her foreign relations India started the idea of non-alignment. This meant that she was not willing to take sides with either party in the big struggles which shake the world. India wanted all disputes to be settled peacefully and she wanted to help in creating friendship

A chemical plant under construction.

between countries. At first this policy was not understood by many. India came in for a lot of abuse. Soon, however, it was realized that India's approach was the only correct one for her, and today non-alignment is practiced by most of the countries of Africa and Asia.

India had to pay a price for her policy. She chose not to have a big army and this left her open to an attack by China in 1962. This was a great shock to the Indians who had treated China as a friend. They now have to spend a lot of their precious resources on an army and weapons to guard against more attacks.

We have been able to touch on only a few of the problems

Like this boy, many people in India do not have enough to eat.

A health worker in an Indian village clinic, preparing to vaccinate a young child. Health workers teach the people about hygiene, as well as providing basic medical care.

and dangers that face India, both internal and external. The country has faced them all with imagination and determination. A happier and more settled people must surely emerge as a result of India's present efforts.

GLOSSARY

Ahimsa   The idea of non-violence advocated by Jainism in the sixth century and later advocated by Mahatma Ghandi.

ashram   School.

Bharat   India.

Buddhism   A religion that follows the teachings of Buddha.

caste system   A system that divides all people into groups according to birth and occupation. People can only associate and marry within their own caste.

Devanagari   Alphabet used in most of the Indian languages.

dhoti   Traditional dress of Indian men.

ghats   Mountain ranges.

Gurkhas   The mountain people of Nepal who are known for their fighting ability.

Himalayas   Mountain chain in India.

Hinduism   A religious group that believes in the supreme god Brahma and many lesser gods.

rajahs   Heads of state in India.

sanskrit   An ancient written language developed by the Aryans who invaded India.

sultans   Heads of state in India.

Vasco da Gama   A Portuguese explorer.

Vedas   Ancient scriptural books.

INDEX

spice trade, 27-30
Sri Lanka, 19
St. George, 30
St. Thomas, 50
stupas, 41
Sudras, 46
suttee, 33
Sryian Christian Church, 50

T

Taj Mahal, 10, 55
Tamil Land, 19
Tamils, 19, 43
Tibet, 17, 18, 21, 23, 25
Tilak, 60
transportation, 93-94
turbans, 83

U

United States, 14, 21
Untouchables, 46-47, 60, 77
Upanishads, 9
Urdu, 88

V

Vaisyas, 46
Varanasi, 90-91
Vedas, 9, 40, 44, 47-48
Victoria, Queen, 36
Vindhya Mountains, 18
Vishnu, 44

Z

Zoroaster, 49